12-7-16

tains

The ... you ... enti!

The Argus

Melbourne, ... Nov 5, 1952
Issue 44

Nelson Mandela Free
50,000 Celebrate in Cape Town

Black Caviar a Sta

LETTERS TO EDITOR

GROOVY! *Lady Bird*
PORTABLE RECORD PLAYER

AVAILABLE NOW! FROM ALL LEADING ...

NUCLEAR EMERGENCY

100,000 evacuated

CRYPTIC CROSSWORD

Goodbye to Astor
Theatre Closes

MENZIES TO TELL PARLIAMENT TODAY

TROOPS TO VIETNAM

Pet of the

Cathy Gets the Gold
Commonwealth Games Victory

with *any* camera...

First Hubble Images
A Long Time Ago...

take
true-to-life
COLOUR PRINTS
morning, noon and night...
Agfacolor
NEGATIVE FILM

NEW YORK CITY

John Lennon Shot

...OTLAND TO VOTE
...re. Naw, Mibbe

...t Everest Conquered
...w Zealand's Pride

Bushfires in Blue

THE NEWS
Today's News Today!

EARTHQUAKE SHAKES STATE

LOTTO RESULTS Page 20

THE WORST SINCE 1900

EXCLUSIVE

Shipboard
a walk to

Charity board sacked over fund allegations

Lady Di in Fatal

"Thanks for the memory."

The Daily Sun
YOUR FIRED

C=64

COMMODORE 64
"THE COMMODORE 64 COULD BE THE MICRO COMPUTER INDUSTRY'S OUTSTANDING NEW PRODUCT INTRODUCTION SINCE THE BIRTH OF THIS INDUSTRY."

Perth girl "Jenny" Best in Show

...s Begin

Reagan vows 'we will go on'

OIL SPILL DISAST
Gulf of Ala

...ins back to ...mal today

Challenger: Final Moments
THE SPACE SHUTTLE DISASTER

THE SUN
SHIRTS

Underarm Bowl Ends Match

Encore CINEMA
CULT & CLASSICS
Casablanca WEDS FRI/SAT 7pm
The Dark Crystal SAT 2pm
Dirty Harry WEDNESDAY MATINEE 12-30pm
Mandolin
BAXTER MON-THURSDAY
QUEEN OF HEARTS
MY LEFT FOOT

ACADEMY TWIN
NOW SHOWING

Flash Floods Fo

Newspaper Hats

To Fa Fa, Nanna Luce, and our newspaper hats. xxx—P.C.

To Pop—O.S.

2016 First US edition
Text copyright © 2015 by Phil Cummings
Illustrations copyright © 2015 by Owen Swan
All rights reserved, including the right of reproduction in whole or in part in any form. Charlesbridge and colophon are registered trademarks of Charlesbridge Publishing, Inc.

Published by Charlesbridge
85 Main Street, Watertown, MA 02472
(617) 926-0329 • www.charlesbridge.com

First published by Scholastic Press, a division of Scholastic Australia Pty Limited, in 2015. This edition published under license from Scholastic Australia Pty Limited.

Library of Congress Cataloging-in-Publication Data
Names: Cummings, Phil, author. | Swan, Owen (Illustrator), illustrator.
Title: Newspaper hats/Phil Cummings; illustrated by Owen Swan.
Description: First US edition. | Watertown, MA: Charlesbridge, 2016.
| 2015 | "First published in Australia by Scholastic Press, a division of Scholastic Australia Pty Limited in 2015." | Summary: A little girl, Georgie, visits her grandfather in the nursing home where he is suffering from memory loss, and manages to reconnect with him when they make newspaper hats for everyone.
Identifiers: LCCN 2015042524 | ISBN 9781580897839 (reinforced for library use) | ISBN 9781632895714 (ebook) | ISBN 9781632895721 (ebook pdf)
Subjects: LCSH: Memory in old age—Juvenile fiction. | Families—Juvenile fiction. | Grandfathers—Juvenile fiction. | Grandparent and child—Juvenile fiction. | Nursing homes—Juvenile fiction. | Newspapers—Juvenile fiction. | CYAC: Memory—Fiction. | Old age—Fiction. | Family life—Fiction. | Grandfathers—Fiction. | Nursing homes—Fiction. | Newspapers—Fiction.
Classification: LCC PZ7.C91482 Ne 2016 | DDC 823.92—dc23 LC record available at http://lccn.loc.gov/2015042524

Printed in China
(hc) 10 9 8 7 6 5 4 3 2 1

Illustrations done in watercolor and pencil on paper
Display type set in Bodoni 72 Oldstyle
Text type set in Granjon
Printed by 1010 Printing International Limited in Huizhou, Guangdong, China
Production supervision by Brian G. Walker
Designed by Sarah Richards Taylor

Newspaper Hats

Phil Cummings

Illustrated by Owen Swan

Charlesbridge

G eorgie walked through the doors that opened like curtains.

"Will Grandpa remember me today?" she asked.
Her father squeezed her hand and smiled. "Wait and see."

Georgie and Dad
walked down corridors
that twisted and turned . . .

until they came to a sky-blue door.

Grandpa's room was full of sunshine.
His collection of old newspapers was stacked
around him like tall city buildings.

"Hi, Grandpa," said Georgie.

Grandpa put his newspaper down.
He looked into Georgie's wide eyes.
"Hello there," was all he said.

"Grandpa," said Georgie, "do you remember me?"

Grandpa looked away
and reached for a
photo on the shelf.
"I remember my brother
and tadpoles in cans,"
he said. "And summer
rain from thunderclouds
that tasted like dust."

"I love the rain in
summer," said Georgie.

"But do you remember me?" she asked.

"I remember my mum in the kitchen,"
said Grandpa. "The fire was warm.
She baked crusty bread and spread
it with butter and honey. The honey
melted all over my fingers."

"I love honey on warm bread, too,"
said Georgie.

"But Grandpa, do you remember me?"

"The rain was hard in the jungle. The chopper blades sliced the air, and wild wind whipped through the trees. I was frightened."

Georgie squeezed Grandpa.
"Don't be frightened, Grandpa."

"Here," said Georgie. "That's me, that's you, and that's Dad. You made me a newspaper hat, remember?"

Grandpa smiled. "I love newspaper hats," he said.

"So do I," said Dad.

"Me, too," said Georgie. "Let's make them now."

Flip . . .

flap . . .

flop . . .

fold.

When the hats were finished, Georgie, Grandpa,
and Dad walked out to the garden.

Georgie helped Grandpa give the hats to his friends.

Mary sang.

Big Bruno clapped.

And the baby bouncing on
Mrs. Carlton's lap giggled.

Suddenly a gust of wind lifted Grandpa's hat and swept it away.

"I'll get it!" Georgie cried.

She jumped,

she twirled,

she skipped,

and she ran.

But she couldn't catch it.

"Don't worry, Grandpa," said Georgie.
"We can make another one."
"Yes," said Grandpa. "I remember how."

tains

The Argus

Melbourne Wed Nov 5 1952

Nelson Mandela Free

50,000 Celebrate
in Cape Town

Black Caviar a Sta

GROOVY! *Lady Bird*

PORTABLE RECORD PLAYER

AVAILABLE NOW! FROM ALL LEADING H.F. RETAILERS

NUCLEAR EMERGENCY

LETTERS TO EDITOR

CRYPTIC CROSSWORD

Goodbye
to Astor
Theatre Closes

MENZIES TO TELL PARLIAMENT TODAY

TROOPS TO VIETNAM

Pet of the Y

100,000 evacuated

Cathy Gets the Gold

Commonwealth
Games Victory

First Hubble Images

A Long Time Ago...

CLASSIFIEDS

John Lennon Shot